SLOMBO THE GROSS

by Rodney A. Greenblat

HarperCollins*Publishers*

Slombo the Gross • Copyright © 1993 by Rodney Alan Greenblat • Printed in the U.S.A. All rights reserved.

Typography by Christine Kettner • # • 10 9 8 7 6 5 4 3 2 1 • First Edition

Library of Congress Cataloging-in-Publication Data • Greenblat, Rodney Alan, date.

Slombo the Gross / by Rodney Alan Greenblat. • p. cm.

Summary: When the Swamp Beast's only food source is threatened and he drives hordes of skunks

into town, only the disgusting Slombo the Gross can restore the ecological balance.

ISBN 0-06-020775-2. — ISBN 0-06-020776-0 (lib. bdg.) • [1. Ecology—Fiction.

2. Monsters—Fiction. 3. Cleanliness—Fiction.] I. Title.

PZ7.G8277SI • 1993 • 91-31235

[E]—dc20 • CIP • AC

For Kimberly and Cleo

Right over by the dump, just behind the dirty part of the highway, lives a truly disgusting guy named Slombo the Gross. Slombo never cleans up, and he hasn't taken a bath since he was three.

Even though he is totally gross, nearly everyone likes him. Slombo's pet cockroaches always have a great time when he is around.

One morning Slombo ran out of gross stuff to eat and decided to go to the grocery store. The cockroaches wanted to go, too, but Slombo said that someone had to stay home and keep the house really messy.

Slombo put on his dirtiest clothes and his completely crushed hat and walked out into the sunshine. The cockroaches were sad to see him go.

Off **Slombo** went, choosing the muddiest path through the dump. A mother sea gull dropped him a couple of worms for a snack. He thanked her but decided to keep them as pets. He named them Hank and Henry.

Even though Slombo had stunk up the whole dump as he passed, the creatures who lived there were sorry that he couldn't stay.

Mrs. Crummy, the schoolteacher, has a hard time teaching when Slombo walks by. The children always forget what they are doing when they see him, and they wave and make gross noises. Slombo likes the schoolchildren.

Mr. Chuck, the owner of the grocery store, does not like Slombo at all. Slombo always causes accidents in the store. This time he knocked over the applesauce.

Just as **Mr. Chuck** and **Skippy**, the checkout boy, began to clean up the applesauce, a loud scream came from outside. This scared **Slombo** so much that he slipped and knocked over the diet soda.

"SKUNKS! SKUNKS!" a woman was screaming outside. Skunks were everywhere, running and stinking up the whole town. No one could catch them, and the police were helpless.

Slombo, having had a pet skunk as a child, knew exactly what to do. By closing his nose and blowing air out of a horn on the top of his head, he could produce the sound of a mother skunk calling her kits.

When the skunks heard it, they were surprised and confused. They stopped their running and gathered around Slombo. The townspeople watched in amazement.

The chief skunk told Slombo that a horrible Swamp Beast had invaded the forest and had threatened to eat them. Slombo wondered why a Swamp Beast would want to go to the forest in the first place.

While the police were still figuring out who would go after the Swamp Beast, Slombo was already on his way. Dripping with sticky diet soda and applesauce, he marched into the woods fearlessly, with his army of worried skunks.

When they reached the darkest part of the forest, they all got hungry. Slombo remembered the pet worms he had in his pocket. He ate Henry and shared Hank with the skunks.

Suddenly there was a terrible roar! The skunks ran for their lives!

Anyone who thought Slombo was disgusting had never met the Swamp Beast. It was slimy and had ten arms and seven eyes. It made an awful slurping noise and smelled like old sneakers stuffed with dead fish.

Pretending not to be afraid, Slombo asked the Swamp Beast why it had left its cozy home in the smelly green swamp and why it was threatening to eat skunks.

Instead of roaring a terrible roar, the Swamp Beast began to cry. "I don't even like skunks," it sobbed. "Somebody has taken all the Tar Gum Nuts from the swamp, and now there's nothing there for me to eat."

Slombo decided they must go to the swamp to find out who would want to steal all the Tar Gum Nuts. The Swamp Beast (whose name was Joey) was afraid to go at first, but Slombo promised to hold one of his ten hands and make everything okay.

When they reached the swamp, they saw men picking what was left of the Tar Gum Nuts and loading them onto a truck.

Slombo and Joey followed the truck to a big factory.
As they peered inside, Slombo figured out what they
were making out of the Tar Gum Nuts.

This!

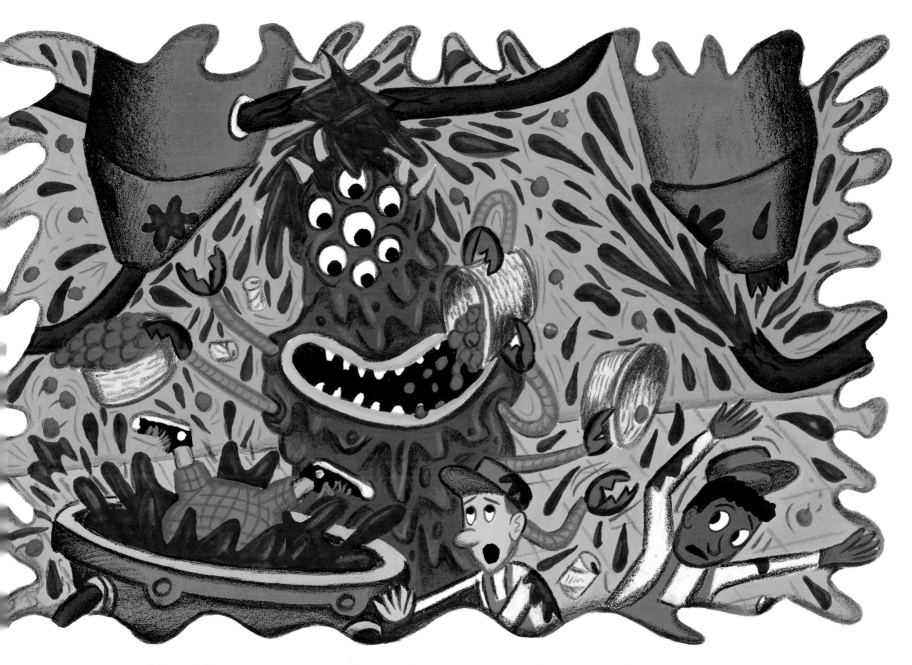

Unable to control himself, Joey burst into the factory and began devouring all the Tar Gum Nuts. The factory workers ran for their lives! In the panic Slombo slipped and fell headfirst into the soda vat.

The next morning at the police station the whole thing got straightened out. The owner of the diet soda company promised to set aside half of all the Tar Gum Nuts for Joey. In return, Slombo promised everyone the skunks would not come into the town again.

EVERYTHING GETS STRAIGHTENED OUT

The mayor was so pleased, she awarded Slombo a certificate of honor. Mr. Chuck presented Slombo with a big bag of junk food and promised him a lifetime of free delivery from the grocery store.

Back at home the cockroaches did not believe Slombo's
amazing story. They were just glad to have him back,
safe and as totally gross as ever.